THE
SUNNIS
OF
LEBANON

A Community in Transition

DR. ABRAHAM KHOUREIS, Ph.D.

:

Copyright Notice

Note & Disclaimer

This book is a work of literature inspired by true events. While it draws from historical accounts, traditions, and collective memory, certain characters, dialogues, and scenes have been adapted for narrative purposes. Although it is based on accurate historical resources, it is not intended to serve as a definitive historical record.

Any resemblance to actual persons, living or deceased, as well as to organizations, institutions, governments, or groups, beyond the well-known historical figures and entities referenced, is entirely coincidental and unintentional.

The purpose of this work is to honor the essence of events and to explore their moral, spiritual, and human significance through the medium of authentic and real storytelling.

:

Lebanon: People and Cultures Series

Lebanon is more than a point on the Mediterranean map; it is a living mosaic of peoples, faiths, and traditions whose encounters, conflicts, and sacrifices have shaped its destiny.

In this honest and thoughtful series, Dr. Abraham Khoureis, Ph.D., a global thinker, leadership scholar, and apostle of compassionate leadership examines Lebanon's communities with clarity and courage, bringing their histories and identities to light.

Each volume explores both the triumphs and the trials of this diverse land:

The Shia of Lebanon: The Guardians of the Nation, celebrating endurance, sacrifice, and their vital role in defending Lebanon's sovereignty.

The Maronites of Lebanon: Identity Crisis, Divided Nation. Confronting the legacy of power and imbalance while recognizing their cultural and educational contributions.

The Druze of Lebanon: The Keepers of The Mountain, unveiling the resilience and spiritual uniqueness of this mountain community.

:

The Sunnis of Lebanon: A Community in Transition, tracing their influence in Lebanon's coastal cities and their links to the wider Arab world.

Future volumes will bring forward the stories of Lebanon's other communities.

Together, these works form a comprehensive account of Lebanon's people and cultures, a portrait both unflinching and compassionate. They speak to leaders, scholars, and citizens alike, reminding the world that Lebanon cannot be understood without acknowledging all its communities.

It is written with the hope that the insights within these pages will guide those in power to safeguard this fragile, divided country, so that Lebanon may yet rediscover unity, dignity, and peace.

Table of Contents

:

"Lebanon is bigger than all of us."

Rafik Hariri

Preface

This book is one volume in a larger effort to understand Lebanon as it truly is, a country shaped not by a single narrative, but by many vibrant communities whose histories intersect, overlap, and at times collide. The Sunnis of Lebanon belongs to the People and Cultures of Lebanon series, a collection devoted to explaining the major communities that together form the Lebanese experience.

Each volume in this series follows the same discipline. It asks a simpler and more demanding question: how did this community form, how did history shape its role, and how did its relationship to power, geography, and institutions influence its present condition?

The Sunni community of Lebanon has often been discussed through the lens of recent politics. In public discourse, it is frequently reduced to moments of absence or failure, or conversely, to assumptions of inherited authority. Both approaches flatten a far more complex history.

This book steps away from immediacy and returns to structure. It examines how Sunnis emerged within systems of governance, administration, and commerce, and how those systems defined both their strengths and their limitations over time.

Like the other volumes in this series, this work resists sectarian storytelling. It avoids nostalgia and avoids accusation. It treats history as a process rather than a verdict. The Sunni presence in Lebanon did not arise from a single origin, a single mission, or a single identity. It developed gradually, shaped by empire, urban life, and institutional continuity.

Understanding that process is essential to understanding the community itself.

In this book I do not ask the reader to agree. I ask you as the reader to see. To read patiently. To allow historical patterns to emerge without interruption. Then, only then can Lebanon's communities be understood not as rivals competing for legitimacy, but as distinct histories sharing the same fragile space. That is the purpose of this volume. And that is the purpose of the series to which it belongs.

Introduction

In Lebanon, few communities are spoken about as frequently and understood as little as the Sunnis. They are often described through their political moments rather than their historical formation, through what they lack today rather than what shaped them over centuries. In public conversation, they appear either as remnants of a lost authority or as passive actors in a system that moved on without them. Both descriptions are incomplete.

This book begins from a different place. It does not start with the present and work backward. It begins with formation, with structure, with the conditions that produced a Sunni presence in Lebanon long before the modern state existed. Only by understanding those foundations can the contemporary condition be approached with clarity rather than judgment.

The Sunni community in Lebanon was never formed as a closed or defensive society. It did not grow around geography that insulated it from authority, nor around institutions designed to resist the state. Instead, it developed in proximity to governance itself. Its identity took shape within administration, law, trade, and urban life. This orientation created stability when power was centralized and continuity was assured. It also created dependency when those structures weakened or collapsed.

Modern discourse often treats Sunni influence as something that was taken away. History suggests something more precise. Sunni influence, where it existed, was rarely autonomous. It was relational. It depended on functioning institutions, recognized authority, and predictable governance. When these eroded, the community did not lose a homeland or a fortress. It lost a framework.

This distinction matters. Communities that anchor themselves in land, kinship, or defensive geography respond to instability differently than those anchored in institutions. The Sunni experience in Lebanon cannot be measured using criteria developed for mountain societies or resistance-based identities. Doing so leads to misinterpretation and misplaced expectations.

In this volume I do not argue that the Sunni path

was superior or flawed. I explain that it was specific. I examine why Sunnis gravitated toward cities, why they became associated with administration and commerce, and why their social organization reflected the logic of empire rather than the logic of autonomy. These patterns were not accidental, nor were they unique to Lebanon. They were consistent across regions where Sunnism aligned with state authority.

As part of the *Lebanon: People and Cultures* series, this book follows the same discipline applied to every community examined. It avoids exceptionalism. It resists moral ranking. It treats each group as a historical outcome rather than a political position. The Sunni community is approached here neither as an actor to be defended nor as a subject to be corrected, but as a community shaped by choices, constraints, and circumstances across centuries.

The chapters that follow trace this development carefully. They move from origins to settlement patterns, from imperial administration to the disruptions of modernity. They examine moments of continuity and moments of fracture, not to assign responsibility, but to explain consequences. The aim is not to resolve present debates, but to provide the context without which those debates remain shallow.

Understanding the Sunnis of Lebanon requires patience. It requires letting go of inherited assumptions and resisting the urge to read history through today's anxieties. In this introduction I invite readers to do exactly that. To read with proportion. To separate structure from sentiment. And to see the Sunni story as one essential thread in Lebanon's larger, unfinished formation.

Chapter 1

Origins and Early Formation

The Sunni presence in Lebanon developed gradually and cannot be traced to a single origin, migration, or founding moment. It emerged within the broader historical context of Bilad al-Sham, a region that for centuries functioned as a continuous political, commercial, and cultural space under successive empires.

Arab presence in the Levant predates Islam by several centuries. By the late Roman and Byzantine periods, Arab tribes were already established in Greater Syria, including groups such as the Ghassanids, who were Christian Arab allies of Byzantium, and other Arab populations operating along trade routes linking the Arabian Peninsula, the Syrian interior, and the Mediterranean coast.

These populations were involved in trade, military service, and frontier administration. Islam did not introduce Arabs to the region, but it shifted political authority toward Arabic language and Arab leadership.

Prior to the Islamic period, the Lebanese coast consisted of established urban centers, notably Beirut, Tripoli, Sidon, and Tyre. These cities functioned as ports and administrative hubs under Roman and Byzantine rule. They collected taxes, administered law, and facilitated maritime trade across the eastern Mediterranean. Their populations were urban in character and accustomed to governance through imperial institutions.

With the new Islamic rule of Greater Syria in the seventh century, these cities were incorporated into the new political order without being dismantled. Administrative authority shifted to Muslim rule, and Arabic gradually replaced Greek and other languages as the primary language of governance.

Over time, local populations embraced Islam through gradual and varied processes. Accepting Islam occurred across generations and was influenced by religious adoption, social integration, access to administrative roles, and participation in the economic life of the state. Arabic language use expanded alongside these developments, reinforcing a process of Arabization that unfolded unevenly across regions and communities.

As Sunni Islam became the dominant legal and religious framework of governance, public institutions reflected that structure. Courts applied Sunni jurisprudence, educational institutions operated within Sunni traditions, and religious endowments were administered accordingly. Urban centers reflected this alignment due to their function as seats of law, administration, and commerce.

Given their historical association with state administration, legal authority, and commerce, Sunni communities gravitated toward Lebanon's urban and commercial centers, where governance and economic life were concentrated. This pattern reflected the organization of imperial rule rather than any deliberate demographic policy.

During later periods, particularly under Mamluk and Ottoman rule, Sunni presence in Lebanese cities was further reinforced. Ottoman administration, which adopted Sunni Islam as its official legal framework, appointed judges, governors, and municipal officials to cities such as Tripoli, Beirut, and Sidon. Trade networks linking these ports to Damascus, Anatolia, Palestine, and

Egypt contributed to continued movement of families, scholars, and merchants. Some Sunni families trace their origins to these regional centers, while others emerged locally through long-standing participation in urban institutions.

The result was an urban Sunni population shaped by sustained association with governance, commerce, and legal authority. Rather than originating from a single ethnic or geographic source, Sunni communities in Lebanon developed as a layered population formed through early conquest, gradual conversion, regional mobility, and institutional continuity.

This early formation established patterns of settlement and social organization that continued to influence the community's position in later historical periods.

Chapter 2

Ottoman Rule and Urban Consolidation

Ottoman rule marked a period of consolidation rather than transformation for Sunni communities in Lebanon. When the Ottomans incorporated Greater Syria in the early sixteenth century, they inherited urban centers that were already administratively organized and socially stratified. Their system did not introduce new patterns of settlement, but it reinforced existing ones.

The Ottoman Empire adopted Sunni Islam as the official legal framework of governance. This alignment shaped the structure of administration throughout the provinces, including the coastal cities of Lebanon. Judicial authority, municipal governance, taxation, and religious endowments were organized through Sunni legal institutions. As a result, Sunni presence in urban centers such as Tripoli, Beirut, Sidon, and Tyre became further institutionalized.

11

Ottoman administration relied on appointed officials rather than hereditary local rule in most urban settings. Judges, governors, tax administrators, and military officers were assigned to cities as part of a centralized bureaucratic system. These appointments created steady movement of Sunni officials and their families across the empire, linking Lebanese cities to administrative centers such as Damascus, Istanbul, and other provincial capitals.

Tripoli functioned as an important provincial center, serving as both a port and an administrative hub for northern regions. Beirut, while initially more limited in political significance, grew in importance over time due to its port and its connections to inland trade routes. Sidon played a similar role in the south, linking coastal commerce with agricultural production in surrounding areas. In each case, Sunni presence reflected the role of these cities within the imperial system rather than independent communal organization.

Urban Sunni families often derived their status from service within Ottoman institutions or from commercial activity tied to imperial trade networks. Religious authority was similarly structured. Sunni scholars, judges, and administrators operated within state-recognized frameworks, and religious endowments were managed through official channels.

This practice reinforced a form of leadership that was institutional rather than autonomous.

At the same time, Ottoman governance allowed for local variation. While Sunni legal authority dominated urban administration, other communities retained autonomy in matters of personal status and local affairs, particularly in mountainous regions. This arrangement further distinguished urban Sunni life from the social organization of communities that developed outside direct state administration.

Throughout the Ottoman period, Sunni communities in Lebanon remained closely associated with cities and with the institutions of governance. Their cohesion depended less on territorial control or kinship networks and more on continuity within administrative, legal, and commercial systems. This orientation provided stability as long as imperial authority remained intact.

By the late Ottoman period, changes in global trade, administrative reform, and increasing European involvement in the eastern Mediterranean began to alter these arrangements. Beirut, in particular, expanded rapidly as a commercial port, drawing increased population and economic activity. Sunni participation in urban administration and commerce continued, but the broader context in which these roles functioned was beginning to shift.

Ottoman rule thus represents a period in which Sunni urban presence in Lebanon was reinforced and normalized within imperial structures. It also laid the groundwork for later challenges, as the community's position remained closely tied to institutions that would eventually be transformed or dismantled with the collapse of the Ottoman empire.

Chapter 3

The French Mandate and Political Reorientation

The collapse of the Ottoman Empire marked a decisive break in the structures that had shaped Sunni life in Lebanon for centuries. With the end of imperial rule after the First World War, the administrative framework within which Sunni communities had long functioned was dismantled. The French Mandate introduced a new political order, one that differed fundamentally in structure, priorities, and sources of legitimacy.

Under the Mandate, Lebanon was separated administratively from the wider Syrian context in which Sunni urban life had historically been embedded. The creation of Greater Lebanon in 1920 altered political geography, placing coastal Sunni cities within a state whose demographic balance and governing philosophy differed from those of the Ottoman system. Authority was no longer derived from a Sunni imperial framework, but from a colonial administration that governed through new institutions and alliances.

French rule reshaped political life through centralized administration and sect-based representation. While Sunnis continued to play roles in municipal governance, commerce, and the professions, their traditional relationship to authority changed. Administrative appointments were no longer primarily tied to Sunni legal and bureaucratic systems. Instead, power flowed through the Mandate structure, which favored new political arrangements and redefined communal roles. The legal system also underwent significant transformation.

Ottoman courts and administrative practices were replaced or modified by French legal frameworks. While religious courts continued to operate in matters of personal status, their role within the broader governance system was reduced. Sunni legal authority, once central to public administration, became more limited in scope.

Economic patterns shifted as well. Beirut expanded as a commercial and administrative center under French rule, benefiting from investment and infrastructure development. Sunni participation in trade, finance, and professional life remained significant, but it now operated within a colonial economy oriented toward European interests rather than imperial integration across the eastern Mediterranean.

Politically, Sunni leadership faced a period of adjustment. The loss of Ottoman structures meant the loss of an established pathway to authority. Sunni elites who had previously derived influence from administrative service now had to navigate representative politics, colonial oversight, and emerging national institutions. This transition was uneven and often uncertain.

The Mandate period also introduced new forms of communal competition. Political representation increasingly took sectarian form, encouraging communities to organize around identity rather than institutional function. For Sunnis, whose historical cohesion had been tied to administration rather than collective mobilization, this shift required adaptation to a political environment that emphasized communal bargaining.

By the end of the Mandate, Sunni communities in Lebanon remained firmly urban and engaged in public life, but their relationship to power had changed. Authority was no longer continuous or assumed. It had become negotiated, contested, and mediated through a state whose foundations differed from those under which Sunni urban life had developed.

The French Mandate thus represents a period of reorientation. It disrupted long-standing institutional alignments and introduced political structures that would shape Sunni participation in the Lebanese state after independence. The consequences of this transition would become more visible in the decades that followed.

Chapter 4

Independence and Early State Formation

Lebanon's independence from France in 1943 introduced a new political framework that differed from both Ottoman administration and French colonial rule. The emerging Lebanese Republic was built on a negotiated system of power-sharing that sought to balance the country's diverse communities through institutional arrangements rather than centralized authority. For Sunni communities, this period marked both continuity and adjustment.

Under the National Pact, political roles were distributed along sectarian lines. The position of Prime Minister was designated for a Sunni Muslim, establishing a formal place for Sunni leadership within the new state. This arrangement reflected the historical association of Sunnis with governance and public administration, but it also placed that role within a system that emphasized communal representation rather than institutional continuity.

Sunni political influence in the early years of independence was concentrated in urban centers, particularly Beirut, Tripoli, and Sidon. Sunni leaders emerged from established families with experience in administration, commerce, and the professions. Their authority was exercised primarily through political office, parliamentary participation, and engagement with state institutions rather than through independent communal structures. The early republic relied heavily on bureaucratic governance and economic activity centered in cities.

Sunni participation in public administration, diplomacy, education, and commerce remained significant. Beirut, in particular, expanded as a regional financial and commercial hub, drawing increased Sunni involvement in banking, trade, and professional services.

At the same time, the new political system required Sunni leaders to operate within a framework of negotiated compromise. Power was shared rather than centralized, and decision-making depended on consensus among communal representatives. This environment differed from earlier periods in which Sunni authority had been embedded within broader imperial systems.

Socially, Sunni communities continued to reflect their urban character. Educational attainment, professional mobility, and engagement with state institutions remained defining features. Religious authority, while present, did not function as a centralized or autonomous structure. Sunni cohesion relied more on political participation and civic engagement than on formal communal organization.

Regional developments also shaped this period. Lebanon's position within the Arab world, particularly its relationship with neighboring Syria and broader Arab nationalism, influenced Sunni political discourse. Sunni leaders often engaged with Arab political movements while operating within the constraints of the Lebanese state.

By the late 1950s, tensions within the political system became more visible. Disagreements over foreign alignment, internal governance, and communal balance highlighted structural vulnerabilities within the state. Sunni participation in these debates reflected both their investment in the republic and the limits of their influence within a system defined by compromise.

The early decades of independence thus represented a period in which Sunni communities maintained a central role in public life while adapting to a new political order. Their influence was institutional and political rather than territorial, shaped by the structures of the Lebanese state and the broader regional environment in which it operated.

Chapter 5

Civil War and Institutional Disruption

The outbreak of the Lebanese civil war in 1975 marked a period of profound disruption for all communities, but it affected Sunni communities in ways closely tied to their historical relationship with the state. As central authority weakened and then collapsed, the institutional framework that had long structured Sunni political and social life ceased to function.

The war fragmented the Lebanese state and dismantled many of its administrative and security institutions. Ministries, courts, and public services either stopped operating or operated in limited form. For Sunni communities, whose cohesion and influence had been largely embedded in state structures, this collapse created an immediate vacuum. Authority shifted away from institutions toward armed groups and localized power centers.

Sunni areas, particularly in Beirut, Tripoli, and Sidon, experienced both physical and political fragmentation. While various Sunni political figures and organizations remained active, they did not coalesce into a unified military or territorial force comparable to those formed by other communities during the conflict. Sunni participation in the war was often mediated through alliances rather than independent structures.

Armed groups operating in Sunni-majority areas were frequently influenced by regional actors, Palestinian organizations, or broader ideological movements rather than by a centralized Sunni leadership. This reflected the absence of a preexisting communal military framework and the continued reliance on external or cross-communal arrangements.

Economic and social life in Sunni urban centers was significantly disrupted. Beirut, once the administrative and commercial heart of the country, was divided and partially destroyed. Trade networks collapsed, public services deteriorated, and large segments of the population were displaced. Sunni professionals, merchants, and civil servants were particularly affected by the breakdown of institutions that had previously sustained their roles.

Politically, Sunni leaders continued to engage in negotiation and mediation throughout the conflict. Their influence was exercised largely through political dialogue, diplomatic engagement, and participation in shifting alliances rather than through direct territorial control. This approach reflected both historical patterns and the constraints imposed by the conflict environment.

The civil war also altered patterns of authority within Sunni communities. With state institutions weakened, informal networks gained greater importance. Local leaders, family connections, and external patrons played increasing roles in providing services and security. This shift, however, did not fully replace the institutional framework that had previously structured Sunni life.

By the end of the war, Sunni communities remained firmly urban and politically engaged, but their relationship to authority had been fundamentally altered. The conflict exposed the vulnerability of a community whose historical strength lay in institutions that no longer functioned as intended.

The civil war thus represents a period in which long-standing patterns of Sunni engagement with the state were disrupted without being replaced by alternative structures. The consequences of this disruption would shape Sunni political and social life in the post-war period.

Chapter 6

Post-War Settlement
Redefining Authority

The end of the civil war and the signing of the Taif Agreement in 1989 marked a formal return to state-centered governance in Lebanon. For Sunni communities, the post-war period represented an attempt to reestablish a relationship with authority after years of institutional collapse, though under conditions that differed significantly from those that existed before the war.

The Taif Agreement rebalanced political power within the Lebanese system. Executive authority was shifted from the presidency to the Council of Ministers, strengthening the role of the Prime Minister. As the office constitutionally designated to a Sunni Muslim, this change appeared, in formal terms, to enhance Sunni political influence within the state. In practice, however, authority became more dispersed and increasingly constrained by external factors.

Post-war reconstruction focused heavily on Beirut and other urban centers. State institutions were rebuilt, ministries reopened, and public administration resumed. Sunni participation in government, public service, and economic life reemerged alongside these efforts. Many Sunni leaders viewed this period as a return to familiar ground, a restoration of governance through institutions rather than through force.

At the same time, the post-war state operated under significant limitations. Syrian influence over Lebanese political life shaped decision-making at the highest levels. While Sunni leaders held formal authority within government, their autonomy was circumscribed by regional power dynamics and security arrangements that lay beyond state institutions.

Economically, the reconstruction period reshaped Sunni urban life. Beirut's redevelopment reinforced its role as a financial and commercial center, drawing Sunni engagement in business, banking, and professional services. This economic revival, however, was uneven. Benefits were concentrated in specific sectors and locations, while broader social challenges persisted.

Politically, Sunni leadership during this period was characterized by centralization around prominent figures rather than broad institutional depth. Authority flowed through political office and personal networks more than through durable communal structures. This reflected both the legacy of the war and the nature of the post-war political environment.

Socially, Sunni communities remained urban and engaged, but signs of fragmentation were visible. Economic disparities widened, and younger generations faced changing conditions that differed from those experienced by earlier Sunni elites. While formal political representation remained intact, the connection between leadership and broader communal life became more complex.

The post-war settlement thus restored a measure of institutional participation for Sunni communities without fully reestablishing the conditions that had previously sustained their role within the state. Authority was present, but it was mediated, constrained, and increasingly dependent on political negotiation rather than administrative continuity.

This period set the stage for new challenges. The foundations of Sunni engagement with the Lebanese state had been reassembled, but they rested on altered ground. The implications of this shift would become clearer in the years that followed.

Chapter 7

The Contemporary Sunni Condition

In the years following the post-war settlement, Sunni communities in Lebanon entered a period marked less by transformation than by uncertainty. The institutional framework that once anchored Sunni political and social life remained in place, but its capacity to generate cohesion and authority steadily weakened.

Sunni political representation continued to operate primarily through the office of the Prime Minister and parliamentary participation. Formal presence within the state persisted, but the ability of political leadership to translate position into broad influence declined. Decision-making increasingly reflected coalition politics, external pressures, and shifting regional dynamics rather than stable institutional authority.

Urban centers remained the core of Sunni life.

Beirut, Tripoli, and Sidon continued to host political, economic, and professional activity. At the same time, economic inequality within these cities became more pronounced. Sections of the Sunni population experienced declining access to opportunity, while established networks retained disproportionate influence. This divergence contributed to growing distance between leadership and broader social realities.

The weakening of centralized authority also affected communal cohesion. Unlike communities structured around territorial control or tightly organized institutions, Sunni communities relied heavily on state frameworks to mediate interests and resolve disputes. As those frameworks lost effectiveness, alternative forms of organization did not fully emerge. Leadership remained fragmented, often reactive rather than directive.

Regional developments further shaped this condition. Shifts in the balance of power in the Middle East, changing relationships with neighboring states, and evolving international engagement all influenced Sunni political positioning. These factors limited the capacity of local leadership to define independent strategies within the Lebanese context.

Social and cultural change added another layer of complexity. Younger generations navigated a landscape shaped by economic constraint, political stagnation, and reduced confidence in public institutions.

Traditional pathways through education, public service, and professional advancement became less reliable, altering expectations that had once defined Sunni urban life.

Despite these challenges, Sunni communities remained deeply integrated into Lebanese society. Participation in civic life, professional sectors, and cultural institutions continued. The absence of cohesive leadership did not translate into disengagement, but rather into diffuse forms of participation without a unifying framework.

The contemporary Sunni condition thus reflects a community still positioned within the state, but no longer anchored by it in the same way as in earlier periods. Authority exists, but it is fragmented. Representation remains, but it lacks depth. The structures that once provided continuity now operate with diminished capacity.

This condition is not the result of a single event or decision. It is the cumulative outcome of historical alignment with institutions that have changed in form and function. Understanding this context is essential to assessing the present without resorting to assumption or blame.

Chapter 8

Future Trajectories Within a Constrained State

The future of Sunni communities in Lebanon is shaped less by choice than by structure. The political, economic, and institutional environment in which Sunnis operate today imposes limits that did not exist in earlier periods. Any assessment of future trajectories must therefore begin with the realities of the Lebanese state itself.

Lebanon's post-war political system remains formally intact but functionally strained. State institutions continue to operate unevenly, with recurring periods of paralysis affecting government formation, legislative activity, and public administration. For Sunni communities, whose historical engagement has been closely tied to institutional governance, this instability constrains the capacity to exercise influence through established channels.

The office of the Prime Minister remains constitutionally significant, but its effectiveness depends on consensus within a fragmented political system. Executive authority is shared among multiple actors, and decision-making is often delayed or blocked by competing interests. As a result, formal representation does not consistently translate into policy direction or administrative continuity. This dynamic limits the ability of Sunni leadership to define long-term strategies within the state.

Demographic and urban realities further shape future possibilities. Sunni populations remain concentrated in major cities, particularly Beirut, Tripoli, and Sidon. These urban centers face persistent challenges, including economic contraction, infrastructure deterioration, and uneven access to public services.

Youth unemployment and outward migration have increased, reducing the availability of professional and administrative pathways that once sustained Sunni urban life.

Education and professional sectors continue to serve as points of engagement, but their role has shifted. Public institutions that previously absorbed educated Sunni professionals have weakened, while private-sector opportunities remain limited by broader economic conditions.

Migration, both regional and international, has become an increasingly common response, affecting demographic continuity and leadership development.

Lebanon's political environment remains sensitive to developments in the wider Middle East. Shifts in regional alliances, economic assistance, and diplomatic engagement shape the operating space available to all Lebanese communities, including Sunnis. These external factors limit the degree to which internal reform or reorganization can occur independently.

At the communal level, Sunni leadership faces the challenge of operating without a single unifying institutional framework. Political figures continue to emerge, but leadership remains fragmented and often situational. Civic organizations, professional associations, and religious institutions provide limited coordination but do not function as comprehensive structures capable of replacing state-centered authority.

Economic participation remains an important avenue for engagement. Sunni involvement in commerce, services, and professional sectors persists, though it is unevenly distributed and constrained by broader economic decline. The capacity of economic activity to generate collective cohesion has diminished as opportunities narrow and inequality increases.

Future trajectories therefore reflect a continuation of existing patterns rather than a decisive shift. Sunni communities remain embedded in the state, urban in character, and institutionally oriented, but the institutions themselves no longer provide stable ground. Adaptation occurs incrementally, through negotiation, professional engagement, and selective migration, rather than through collective reorganization.

The direction ahead is neither predetermined nor unified. It is shaped by the interaction of institutional limits, demographic trends, economic conditions, and regional pressures. Understanding these factors provides context for the possibilities available, without presuming outcomes or assigning intent.

Chapter 9

Power, Patronage, and Structural Concentration

Historically, Sunni influence in Lebanon was distributed across institutions rather than concentrated in a single center. Authority flowed through administration, commerce, education, and political office, often shared among multiple families and professional networks. This dispersion reflected the community's long-standing integration within state structures rather than reliance on centralized leadership.

During the Ottoman and early post-independence periods, Sunni public life was shaped by a range of families whose influence derived from service, trade, or professional standing. These families did not function as dynasties in the territorial or military sense. Their authority was situational, tied to office, reputation, and institutional participation. Leadership was plural, and succession was not automatic.

The post-war period introduced a different dynamic. Reconstruction, regional realignments, and the weakening of state institutions altered how influence was exercised. External financial support and political backing began to play a larger role in shaping leadership structures. Within this environment, power became increasingly centralized.

Saudi Arabia emerged as a significant external actor during this phase. Its involvement was expressed primarily through political support, economic assistance, and patronage networks rather than direct intervention in Lebanese governance. Saudi engagement aligned with efforts to stabilize Lebanon after the civil war and to support Sunni political leadership within the framework of the Lebanese state.

This external support interacted with local conditions in ways that reshaped Sunni political life. Financial resources enabled rapid reconstruction and facilitated the rise of centralized leadership figures. At the same time, reliance on external backing introduced new dependencies and reduced the role of traditional institutional pathways.

The emergence of Rafik Hariri marked a decisive shift. Hariri's influence was built on a combination of personal wealth, international connections, reconstruction leadership, and political office.

His role concentrated Sunni political authority in ways not previously seen. Decision-making, representation, and patronage increasingly flowed through a single leadership center.

This concentration altered internal dynamics. Traditional Sunni families and professional networks remained present, but their roles were redefined. Influence became more closely tied to proximity to centralized leadership rather than to institutional position alone. Political participation shifted from dispersed engagement to alignment with dominant figures.

Hariri's tenure also reshaped the relationship between Sunni leadership and the state. Reconstruction efforts reinforced Beirut's centrality and reasserted the role of the Prime Minister's office as a focal point of governance. At the same time, institutional depth did not expand at the same pace as political authority, leaving leadership structures vulnerable to disruption.

Following Hariri's assassination, the limitations of concentrated power became more visible. The absence of a comparable unifying figure exposed gaps in leadership continuity. Authority fragmented, and competing actors emerged without a shared institutional framework to coordinate them. External support remained influential, but it no longer produced the same degree of cohesion.

Saudi Arabia's role evolved accordingly. Engagement continued, but with shifting priorities and varying levels of involvement. Sunni political life increasingly reflected regional uncertainty and internal fragmentation rather than centralized direction.

The combined effect of these developments was a redefinition of Sunni leadership. Power moved from dispersed institutional participation toward centralized patronage and then toward fragmentation. This sequence differed from earlier historical patterns and introduced structural challenges that continue to shape the contemporary condition.

Chapter 10

Continuity, Change, and Place Within Lebanon

The Sunni experience in Lebanon is best understood not through moments of prominence or decline, but through patterns that have persisted across centuries. From early formation to the present, Sunni communities have been shaped by proximity to governance, engagement with institutions, and concentration in urban centers. These features did not guarantee dominance, nor did they ensure vulnerability. They defined a particular way of existing within the Lebanese landscape.

Across historical periods, Sunni life was rarely organized around territory or communal insulation. Instead, it was developed within administrative systems, legal frameworks, and commercial networks that extended beyond local boundaries. This orientation allowed Sunni communities to function effectively when authority was centralized and institutions were stable. It also meant that periods of political disruption had disproportionate impact.

What has remained consistent is the urban character of Sunni communities. Beirut, Tripoli, and Sidon have continued to serve as centers of political participation, economic activity, and social life. Even as conditions changed, the connection to cities and to public institutions endured. This continuity distinguishes the Sunni experience from that of communities whose cohesion was rooted more firmly in geography or autonomous structures.

What has changed is the nature of authority itself. Empire, colonial administration, and the early Lebanese state each provided frameworks within which Sunni participation had predictable pathways. The erosion of these frameworks altered the conditions under which influence could be exercised. Institutional roles remained, but their effectiveness declined as the state's capacity weakened.

The post-war period introduced new dynamics that departed from historical patterns. Central leadership, reliance on external patronage, and personalization of authority replaced dispersed institutional participation. While this shift produced temporary cohesion, it lacked durability.

The absence of strong, resilient institutions made continuity difficult once central figures were no longer present.

Today, Sunni communities remain embedded in Lebanon's political and social fabric. Representation persists, engagement continues, and participation in civic and professional life remains significant. At the same time, leadership fragmentation, economic constraint, and institutional weakness limit the ability to translate presence into collective direction.

This condition should not be understood as failure or decline in isolation. It reflects broader transformations within the Lebanese state and regional environment. Sunni communities have been shaped by these forces rather than standing apart from them. Their experience reflects the challenges faced by a state struggling to reconcile pluralism with effective governance.

Within the context of Lebanon's diversity, the

Sunni community occupies a distinct place. It is integral to the country's formation and evolution. Understanding this role requires attention to structure rather than sentiment, to process rather than event.

This volume, like the others in the series, does not offer prescriptions. It offers context. It situates one community within the shared history of a country whose identity has always been collective, contested, and incomplete. The Sunnis of Lebanon are part of that story, shaped by it and contributing to it, in ways that cannot be reduced to moments or personalities alone.

Chapter 11

Structural Lessons and Historical Balance

Looking across the Sunni experience in Lebanon from formation to the present, certain structural patterns emerge with consistency. These patterns do not belong to ideology or leadership style. They belong to the way communities interact with power, institutions, and geography over time.

The Sunni presence in Lebanon was shaped early by proximity to governance and participation in state structures. This orientation produced stability when authority was centralized and institutions functioned predictably. It also meant that Sunni cohesion depended less on land, kinship, or autonomous organization and more on the continuity of administrative systems.

When institutions were strong, Sunni influence was visible and effective. When institutions weakened, that influence diminished without being replaced by alternative frameworks. This pattern repeated

47

across imperial collapse, colonial transition, civil conflict, and post-war reconstruction. It is not a story of loss alone, but of dependence on systems that changed form faster than the community could adapt.

Another consistent feature is the urban character of Sunni life. Cities offered access to education, commerce, and administration, but they also exposed communities to political volatility, economic fluctuation, and external intervention. Urban integration created opportunities while limiting insulation. This dual reality shaped Sunni experience in ways that differed from communities anchored in more autonomous environments.

Leadership structures evolved in response to these conditions. Centralized leadership emerged under specific historical circumstances, particularly in the post-war era, supported by external resources and reconstruction priorities. Neither model proved fully durable in the absence of strong institutions capable of sustaining continuity beyond individuals.

External actors influenced Sunni political life at various points, most notably during the post-war period. Their involvement interacted with local structures rather than replacing them. External support amplified existing dynamics but did not resolve underlying institutional fragility. When conditions shifted, reliance on external alignment revealed its limits.

What distinguishes the Sunni experience is not absence of agency, but the form it took. Agency was exercised through participation rather than control, through negotiation rather than mobilization, and through institutions rather than territory. These choices shaped outcomes without guaranteeing protection against disruption.

Placed within Lebanon's broader mosaic, the Sunni community illustrates a broader lesson about state-centered identities. Communities that grow within institutions are deeply affected when those institutions weaken. Their challenge is not one of legitimacy, but of structural recalibration.

In this chapter I clarified the conditions under which certain approaches succeed or fail. In doing so, it reinforces the central premise of this volume and the series as a whole: that understanding Lebanon requires attention to structure before judgment.

The Sunni experience, viewed in this light, is neither anomalous nor isolated. It is an expression of how history, national governance, and social organization intersect over time. Recognizing this allows the past to be read with proportion and the present to be assessed with restraint.

Chapter 12

The Sunnis Within Lebanon's Shared Space

Lebanon's communities have never existed in isolation, and the Sunni experience cannot be understood apart from the broader social and political environment in which it unfolded. Historically, Sunni communities interacted continuously with other groups, through governance, commerce, education, and everyday urban life. These interactions shaped the structure of the Lebanese state itself.

Sunni participation in public life was historically embedded in institutions designed to serve diverse populations. Courts, municipalities, ports, schools, and markets brought communities into regular contact with one another.

Sunni administrators, professionals, and merchants operated within systems that required negotiation, and cooperation across communal lines. This

51

created patterns of coexistence rooted less in ideology than in necessity.

Sunnis occupied designated roles within the Lebanese political system that merger in the twentieth century, particularly in executive governance. These roles did not grant unilateral authority. They required constant engagement with other partners from other communities, reinforcing a political culture based on balance rather than dominance.

Periods of conflict disrupted these arrangements, but they did not erase them. Even during times of fragmentation, Sunni communities remained connected to national processes through political negotiation, economic activity, and civic participation. Their engagement reflected an assumption, sometimes strained but persistent, that stability depended on shared institutions rather than separation.

In the post-war period, challenges to governance affected all communities, not only Sunnis. Institutional weakness, economic decline, and external pressures reshaped how Lebanese society functioned as a whole. Sunni experiences during this period reflected broader national conditions, highlighting the interconnectedness of communal trajectories.

This shared space remains central to understanding the Sunni position in Lebanon today. Sunni communities continue to participate in national life through education, commerce, culture, and public service. While leadership structures face limitations, integration within the country's social and institutional fabric endures.

The Sunni experience thus contributes to a larger understanding of Lebanon as a negotiated society. Communal identities exist alongside shared realities, and historical patterns intersect rather than diverge completely. No community's history can be separated from the country's collective experience.

The final reflection on this chapter places the Sunni community where it has long existed, within Lebanon's common space, shaped by interaction, adaptation, and coexistence. It reinforces that Lebanon is best understood not through isolated narratives, but through the relationships that bind its people together.

Chapter 13

Where They Fell Short, and What Comes Next

To speak frankly about the Sunnis of Lebanon requires acknowledging not only what shaped them, but also where they fell short. It is a necessary reckoning, because communities, like nations, do not stagnate by accident. They stagnate when adaptation lags behind reality.

The first failure was one of overconfidence in permanence. For decades, Sunnis believed that institutions would endure simply because they always had. The courts, the ministries, the bureaucracy, the civil service, these were seen as fixtures rather than fragile constructions. When the state began to weaken, the response was hesitation rather than reform. Trust lingered longer than conditions justified.

A second failure lay in leadership renewal. Sunni leadership became concentrated, personalized, and eventually brittle. The earlier model, dispersed across families, professions, and civic roles, gave way to a narrower center of gravity. When that center collapsed or lost credibility, there was no prepared generation to step in. The vacuum that followed was not ideological, it was structural.

There was also a failure to redefine influence. As Lebanon's political system shifted toward negotiation, leverage, and external sponsorship, Sunni leadership remained anchored to formal legitimacy. While others adapted to informal power, parallel structures, or alternative sources of authority, Sunnis continued to rely on the language of the state, even when the state no longer spoke with force.

Silence, at times, became another weakness. Prudence is valuable, but excessive restraint can drift into absence. In moments that demanded recalibration, the community often waited for consensus that never came. The result was disengagement disguised as patience.

These failures must be understood in context. They did not arise from neglect or malice. They emerged from loyalty to a system that no longer functioned as it once did. What failed was not commitment to

Lebanon, but the assumption that Lebanon would continue to operate as before. The future, however, is not closed.

The Sunni community still holds assets that matter. Urban presence remains strong. Education levels remain high. Civic sensibility endures. The idea of public life, though bruised, has not disappeared. These are not small foundations.

What the future requires is recalibration rather than reinvention. Influence can no longer depend solely on institutions that exist only in form. Leadership must broaden again, drawing from professionals, local figures, and independent voices rather than singular centers of power. Engagement must become adaptive, able to operate within weakness without surrendering principle.

Most importantly, the future requires clarity. A community cannot navigate transition without understanding its own limits. The Sunnis of Lebanon must recognize that legitimacy alone is insufficient without leverage, and participation alone cannot substitute for vision.

Lebanon itself remains unfinished. Its political order is unstable, its economy fractured, its institutions strained. In such an environment, no community can thrive in isolation. The Sunni future is inseparable from the country's ability to restore credibility, coherence, and trust.

The Sunnis of Lebanon stand at such a moment. Not diminished beyond recovery, and not immune to further decline. What happens next depends not on nostalgia for what was lost, but on the courage to engage differently with what is.

Chapter 14

Implications for the Lebanese State

The transition of the Sunni community cannot be separated from the condition of the Lebanese state. The two have evolved in parallel for decades, shaped by the same structural pressures and institutional constraints. Understanding the Sunni transition therefore offers insight into the broader challenges facing Lebanon as a political system.

Historically, Sunni participation contributed to the functioning of the state through administration, law, and public service. This role supported a model in which authority was exercised through institutions rather than through territorial control or communal autonomy. When these institutions operated with consistency, they provided a framework that benefited not only Sunnis, but the state as a whole.

As institutional capacity weakened, this model

became harder to sustain. The erosion of administrative authority reduced the effectiveness of governance and altered how political roles functioned. The Sunni transition reflects this shift. Formal representation remains, but institutional depth has declined, limiting the state's ability to act cohesively.

This condition has implications beyond one community. A state in which institutional participation no longer produces stability becomes increasingly reliant on negotiation, external mediation, and short-term arrangements. This dynamic affects all communities, but it is particularly visible in those historically tied to state-centered governance.

The weakening of institutions also changes expectations. Public trust in governance declines when authority appears fragmented or ineffective. Political participation becomes reactive rather than programmatic. Leadership focuses on managing crises rather than shaping long-term policy. These patterns have become features of Lebanese political life.

From this perspective, the Sunni transition highlights a structural imbalance. The state continues to rely on communal representation, but lacks the institutional strength needed to support that system. This imbalance places pressure on communities whose engagement depends on effective governance.

The implications are not limited to politics. Economic management, public services, education, and infrastructure all reflect the same institutional strain. As these systems weaken, social cohesion becomes harder to maintain, and migration increases across communities. The Sunni experience mirrors this national trajectory rather than diverging from it.

The Sunni transition is one expression of a wider reality in which institutions no longer provide the continuity they once did. Understanding this relationship clarifies why community transitions in Lebanon cannot be addressed in isolation. Stability depends less on redistributing roles and more on restoring institutional function. Without that foundation, representation remains symbolic rather than effective.

The Lebanese state and its communities remain interdependent. The transition of one reflects the condition of the other. Recognizing this connection allows for a clearer reading of the present and avoids explanations that reduce complex structural issues to communal narratives.

This understanding completes the analytical arc of the volume. It situates the Sunni transition within Lebanon's shared condition and reinforces the central premise of this series: that Lebanon's future is inseparable from the strength and credibility of its institutions.

"No sect can abolish another sect in Lebanon."

Sheikh Hassan Khaled

Chapter 15

A Community at a Turning Point

By the time Lebanon entered its most recent cycle of collapse, the Sunni community was already standing at a quiet crossroads. The signs were not dramatic. There were no sudden breaks, no sharp declarations, no mass withdrawal. What existed instead was a growing sense that familiar paths no longer led where they once did.

For much of Lebanon's modern history, Sunnis understood themselves through participation. The state was not simply a political structure, it was a shared project. Ministries, courts, schools, and public offices were spaces where presence translated into purpose. Influence was earned through service, and legitimacy flowed from institutions that, while imperfect, still functioned.

As those institutions weakened, the ground beneath that understanding began to shift. Engagement remained, but its meaning changed. Holding office no longer guaranteed influence. Professional achievement no longer ensured stability. The idea that effort would be rewarded by continuity slowly faded, replaced by uncertainty and caution.

This was not a failure of commitment. It was a failure of alignment. The Sunni community continued to relate to the state as though it were intact, even as its capacity eroded. Loyalty endured longer than effectiveness. Trust outlived evidence.

Leadership reflected this tension. Where influence had once been dispersed across families, professions, and cities, it gradually narrowed. Centralization brought visibility, but it also reduced depth. When disruption arrived, continuity proved fragile. The absence that followed was not ideological, it was structural.

Economic pressure sharpened the transition. Urban centers that once sustained Sunni life through commerce and public service struggled under decline. The middle ground thinned. Younger generations encountered blocked pathways and uncertain futures. Migration became a calculation rather than a dream. Those who remained adapted quietly, often disengaging from public life not out of apathy, but out of realism.

Religious institutions faced their own adjustment. Long accustomed to operating alongside the state, they found themselves navigating a landscape where authority was fragmented and coherence harder to maintain. Their presence remained visible, but their capacity to unify or guide diminished. This was not radical change, but dispersion.

What emerged from these shifts was not collapse, but transition. A condition marked by hesitation, reassessment, and uneven adaptation. The Sunni community did not abandon Lebanon, nor did it retreat entirely from public life. It recalibrated, often without a clear map.

This chapter does not seek to assign fault. It seeks to describe a moment. A moment when inherited assumptions no longer hold, and new ones have yet to fully form. A moment when restraint risks being mistaken for absence, and patience for irrelevance.

Understanding this turning point is essential, not because it explains everything that followed, but because it clarifies why certainty gave way to ambiguity. Transition, once recognized, becomes something that can be navigated rather than endured blindly.

DR. ABRAHAM KHOUREIS, PH.D.

The chapters that follow do not resolve this condition. They explore its consequences, its pressures, and its possibilities. Because what the Sunnis of Lebanon face today is not an ending, but an unsettled passage, shaped as much by what remains as by what has been lost.

Chapter 16

The Cost of Waiting

The Sunni experience in Lebanon has long been shaped by restraint. It was not an accidental posture, nor was it born of fear. It emerged from proximity to the state, from an understanding that stability in Lebanon depended on moderation more than confrontation. When one lives inside institutions, one learns that loudness can fracture what little coherence exists.

For decades, Sunnis trusted that patience would protect space. Silence was not withdrawal. It was a calculated discipline, grounded in the belief that the state, even when strained, remained the only legitimate framework through which influence could endure. This belief shaped leadership behavior, public engagement, and political tone.

But restraint carries risk when conditions change. As Lebanon's political system shifted from legitimacy to leverage, silence lost its protective function. What once preserved relevance began to erode it. Appeals to law, procedure, and continuity no longer constrained power as they once had. In this new environment, restraint was often misread, by others and sometimes by Sunnis themselves, as absence.

The difficulty was not knowing when to speak, but knowing how to adapt a language that no longer resonated. Loudness did not align with Sunni instincts, yet quiet participation increasingly failed to register. This produced a prolonged hesitation, a period where engagement continued in form but weakened in effect.

Leadership reflected this tension. As influence narrowed and centralized, visibility increased but depth declined. Renewal stalled. Younger figures found few pathways upward. Authority became attached to circumstance rather than structure. When disruption came, continuity proved fragile.

Understanding this cost is essential. Silence is not inherently weakness, but when context shifts, discipline must evolve. Restraint that does not adapt becomes surrender by default, even when intention remains principled.

Chapter 17

Fragmented Community and External Influence

What is often described as Sunni fragmentation is spread unevenly across cities, generations, and experiences as the structures that once absorbed difference weakened.

Beirut, Tripoli, Sidon, and smaller urban centers now inhabit different realities. Economic pressure, access to opportunity, and political relevance vary sharply. The shared civic framework that once unified experience has thinned, leaving each locality to navigate decline in its own way.

Youth feel this shift most acutely. They inherited an identity rooted in civic participation but encountered a reality where effort no longer guarantees outcome. Education still matters, but no longer ensures stability. Public service still exists, but rarely rewards loyalty. Many respond by disengaging quietly, redefining belonging on personal rather than collective terms.

Religion enters this space not as ideology, but as language. When civic vocabulary loses power, spiritual vocabulary gains presence. This does not signal a radical transformation of identity. It reflects a search for meaning in an environment where public life feels inaccessible. Sunni religious life today is marked more by diversity than direction, presence rather than cohesion.

At the same time, internal differences have sharpened. Elite leadership and popular sentiment drift apart. Religious and political voices operate in parallel rather than in concert. This is not the result of doctrinal division, but of structural absence. Without institutions capable of absorbing difference, diversity hardens into separation.

Faith, once intertwined with civic life, now struggles to reconnect with it. Youth, searching for purpose, find few bridges between belief and public engagement. This gap explains much of the current uncertainty, and much of the quiet frustration that runs beneath the surface.

External influence once provided Sunni leadership with reinforcement. Saudi Arabia played a central role in post-war confidence, reconstruction, and political alignment. As that role diminished, a vacuum formed.

No alternative actor replaced it fully. Engagement became episodic, conditional, and uncertain.

This absence did not cause collapse, but it exposed dependence. Leadership accustomed to sponsorship found itself navigating without anchors. Adjustment became unavoidable, but fragmentation deepened in the absence of a shared framework.

Economic pressure compounded this reality. Urban decline, shrinking middle classes, unemployment, and informal economies reshaped daily life. Politics became transactional. Trust became temporary. Long-term planning gave way to survival thinking. The state remained present, but unreliable.

Yet within this strain lies possibility. Dependence receding creates space for recalibration. The future will not mirror the past. It will demand resilience rather than reliance, realism rather than nostalgia.

What remains is not insignificant. Urban presence endures. Education still matters. Professional competence persists. The memory of institutional life, though bruised, has not vanished. These are foundations, even if they no longer guarantee outcomes.

The path forward will not come through spectacle or withdrawal. It will require adaptive participation, broader leadership, and clarity about limits. Influence can no longer depend solely on institutions that exist in form alone, yet abandoning them would mean surrendering identity itself.

Lebanon remains unfinished. Its political order is fragile, its economy strained, its institutions uneven. No community can stabilize alone, and no state can recover without communities willing to engage realistically rather than romantically.

This transition is not an ending. It is exposure. What emerges will depend not on reclaiming what was lost, but on understanding what no longer works, and acting without illusion.

The Sunnis of Lebanon are not disappearing. They are repositioning, unevenly and imperfectly, within a country still searching for coherence. Their story, like Lebanon's, continues not as a resolved chapter, but as an unfolding one.

Chapter 18

Religious Authority
Weight of Transition

For much of Lebanon's history, Sunni religious authority occupied a careful and restrained position within public life. It functioned alongside the state rather than above it, reinforcing order without seeking dominance. Institutions such as Dar al-Fatwa were never designed to mobilize mass politics or compete for power. Their purpose was quieter, regulating personal status, guiding religious practice, and lending moral legitimacy to a civic order anchored in law and institutions. The Mufti's role was historically one of balance rather than command, presence rather than force.

As the Lebanese state weakened, expectations placed upon religious institutions began to shift. What had once been complementary was increasingly treated as compensatory. Religious authority was asked, implicitly and sometimes explicitly, to fill gaps left by failing governance.

This was not a role it was built to assume. The resulting tension was not between religion and politics, but between responsibility and capacity. Sunni religious leadership remained present, yet cautious, aware that overreach would fracture credibility rather than restore cohesion. Restraint, in this context, reflected continuity rather than failure.

This same restraint shaped the broader Sunni public experience. The community's relationship with the state was once grounded in confidence. Ministries mattered. Courts functioned with enough regularity to command respect. Public office carried authority beyond title. Participation translated into influence.

Today, engagement continues, but expectations are markedly lower. Authority exists in form, but often fails in outcome. This erosion does not produce rebellion. It produces fatigue. Sunnis remain attached to the idea of the state, even as they adjust to its limitations. This distinction is critical. Withdrawal has not occurred. Disillusionment has.

The effects of this shift are felt most sharply by the younger generation. Sunni youth inherited an identity shaped by institutions that no longer function as promised. Education remains valued and ambition persists, yet the pathways that once absorbed graduates into public service, professional life, or stable employment have narrowed sharply. Transition is not theoretical for them. It is lived daily through uncertainty, stalled opportunity, and delayed adulthood. Migration has become a rational choice rather than a last resort.

Political disengagement is often mistaken for apathy, when it is more accurately a response to limited returns on participation.

What Sunni youth experience is not identity loss, but identity mismatch. They were prepared for a system that no longer exists. Civic belonging was framed around institutions that now struggle to deliver. How this generation adapts to that gap will shape the future of the community more decisively than any political figure or external alliance.

Economic pressure has intensified this condition. Urban Sunni life was long sustained by a middle class rooted in commerce, services, and administration. That foundation has thinned. Beirut, Tripoli, and Sidon increasingly reflect inequality, informal economies, and declining opportunity. Economic displacement reshapes political behavior quietly. When survival replaces aspiration, engagement becomes transactional. Fragmentation follows not as a moral failure, but as an economic consequence. Local realities diverge, and shared experience erodes.

Within this environment, questions of identity and authority become more complex. Sunni political Islam has never achieved the dominance in Lebanon that it has elsewhere. Civic identity, tied to plural coexistence and state participation, remained historically stronger. This balance has been tested but not overturned. As institutions weakened, alternative narratives gained visibility, yet not consensus. Most Sunnis continue to distinguish between religious values and political authority. The tension is real, but the community's civic orientation endures.

External dynamics have further reshaped this landscape. Saudi Arabia once served as the primary external reference point for Sunni leadership, particularly in the post-war period. That role has shifted significantly. Regional realignments, reduced engagement, and changing priorities left a vacuum not fully filled by any single actor. Turkey, Western disengagement, and broader regional uncertainty now form a diffuse backdrop rather than a guiding framework. The result is not replacement, but recalibration, and a greater burden of internal responsibility.

Taken together, these forces define the current Sunni condition in Lebanon. Religious authority remains restrained. Youth navigate uncertainty. The state inspires attachment without confidence. Economic pressure fragments experience. External anchors have loosened. What emerges is not collapse, but transition, uneven, unresolved, and ongoing.

"The state is not a tool for enrichment, but a trust that must be protected."

Salim El-Hoss

Chapter 19

Salim El-Hoss
and the Ethics of the State

Salim El-Hoss never fit comfortably into Lebanon's political mythology. He did not rule through charisma, lineage, or spectacle. He did not dominate headlines, mobilize crowds, or cultivate personal loyalty. In a political culture often shaped by visibility and force, El-Hoss represented something quieter, and therefore harder to sustain, the idea that the state itself should matter more than the individual who governs it.

An economist by training, El-Hoss approached politics as administration rather than performance. His understanding of leadership was rooted in balance sheets, institutions, and restraint. He believed that governance was a responsibility to be managed, not a stage to be occupied. This alone placed him at odds with much of Lebanon's political environment.

El-Hoss served multiple times as Prime Minister during some of the country's most difficult periods, including years of civil war and institutional fragmentation. His governments often operated under constraint, sometimes without full authority, sometimes in parallel with rival centers of power. Even in these conditions, his commitment to legality and institutional continuity remained consistent.

What distinguished El-Hoss was not effectiveness measured by outcomes, but integrity measured by limits. He refused to accumulate wealth through office. He avoided political patronage. He declined to turn governance into personal capital. In doing so, he embodied a form of Sunni leadership rooted in principle rather than leverage.

This posture, however, came at a cost. In a system increasingly driven by power rather than procedure, El-Hoss appeared out of step. His insistence on legality was often interpreted as weakness. His refusal to play transactional politics limited his influence. Yet this misreading says more about the system than about the man.

El-Hoss represented an older Sunni instinct, that legitimacy flows from the state, not from its circumvention. He believed that the erosion of institutions was not a temporary inconvenience, but an existential threat to Lebanon itself. Where others adapted by negotiating around the state, he remained loyal to its form, even as its substance weakened.

This loyalty placed him in quiet contrast to later models of Sunni leadership that relied more heavily on external backing, economic power, or centralized authority. El-Hoss did not oppose these models openly, but his presence served as an implicit critique. He demonstrated that one could govern without enrichment, speak without incitement, and lead without spectacle.

In the broader Sunni narrative, El-Hoss occupies a singular place. He reflects both the strength and the vulnerability of a community deeply invested in institutions. His career illustrates what happens when ethics outpace leverage, and when principle confronts a system that no longer rewards it.

El-Hoss legacy should not be misunderstood as failure. It is a record of fidelity. Fidelity to the idea that the state matters, even when it is weak. The public office is service, not opportunity. That restraint is not absence, but choice.

As Lebanon continues its long transition, Salim El-Hoss stands as a reminder of what Sunni leadership once aspired to be, institutional, ethical, and measured. Whether such leadership can reemerge depends less on individuals than on whether Lebanon itself rediscovers the value of the state he never stopped believing in.

Chapter 20

Shared Ground: Sunnis and Lebanon's Other Communities

The Sunni community in Lebanon has never existed in isolation. Its history, influence, and vulnerabilities have always been shaped by its relationship with other Lebanese communities, particularly the Shia, the Druze, and the Christians. These relationships were not static alliances or permanent rivalries. They were negotiated, recalibrated, and often strained by the changing nature of the Lebanese state itself.

What distinguishes Sunni intercommunal relations is that they were rarely built on territorial separation or confessional autonomy. Sunnis lived largely in mixed cities and coastal centers, Beirut, Tripoli, Sidon, where interaction was unavoidable and coexistence was practical rather than ideological. This urban proximity fostered familiarity, cooperation, and competition at the same time.

The Sunni–Christian relationship has historically been anchored in the idea of the Lebanese state. From independence onward, Sunnis and Maronite Christians shared a mutual investment in governance, institutions, and international legitimacy. The National Pact reflected this understanding, Christians securing Lebanon's distinct political identity, Sunnis affirming its Arab belonging.

This partnership functioned as long as institutions carried authority. Sunni participation in government complemented Christian dominance in state architecture. Tensions emerged not from daily coexistence, but from imbalances in power and representation as demographics and regional realities shifted.

In the post-war period, this relationship weakened. While cooperation continued at the elite level, shared vision diminished. Today, Sunni–Christian relations are characterized less by rivalry than by parallel disillusionment. Both communities remain invested in the idea of the state, even as they recognize its fragility.

Recent years have reinforced this convergence of frustration. Economic collapse, institutional paralysis, and emigration have affected Christian and Sunni urban populations deeply. What once separated their political positions now often unites their concerns, though without a coherent joint project.

The Sunni–Druze relationship has been marked by pragmatism rather than ideology. Historically, Druze leadership prioritized autonomy and survival, while Sunnis prioritized continuity through governance. These differing instincts produced tension at times, but also mutual respect.

In moments of crisis, Sunnis and Druze often found common ground through mediation rather than confrontation. Druze leaders frequently acted as brokers, while Sunnis leaned toward institutional solutions. Neither community sought dominance over the other. Their relationship was shaped more by geography and political calculation than by confessional rivalry.

In contemporary Lebanon, this relationship remains relatively stable, though quieter than before. Both communities recognize their limited leverage in a polarized environment.

Coordination occurs episodically, particularly around preserving civil peace, but without strategic alignment. What binds them today is not ambition, but caution.

The Sunni–Shia relationship in Lebanon is the most complex and most frequently misinterpreted. Historically, it was not defined by sectarian hostility. Sunnis and Shia lived alongside one another in cities and villages, connected through trade, labor, and shared social life. Political divergence emerged primarily through differing relationships with power.

Sunnis aligned themselves with the state, believing institutions offered stability and protection. Shia communities, historically marginalized within those institutions, developed parallel structures to secure representation and security. This divergence deepened after the civil war, particularly with the rise of Hezbollah as a dominant Shia political and military force.

The tension between Sunnis and Shia today is less theological than structural. Sunnis continue to measure legitimacy through the state, even as its authority wanes. Shia political power increasingly operates outside the state, while also influencing it. This asymmetry produces frustration rather than open conflict.

Current events have intensified this dynamic. Regional wars, economic collapse, and the paralysis of central authority have placed the Sunni community in a position of restraint while Shia leadership exercises decisive leverage. Sunnis have largely avoided confrontation, not out of fear, but out of concern that escalation would destroy what remains of the state.

At the same time, Sunni–Shia coexistence at the social level has endured. Markets function. Neighborhoods remain mixed. Daily life continues with far less hostility than political rhetoric suggests. This disconnect between elite narratives and lived reality remains one of Lebanon's defining moments.

What emerges from these intercommunal relationships is a mutual restraint. Lebanon today survives less through agreement than through mutual recognition of limits. Sunnis play a central role in this equilibrium. Their instinct to avoid rupture, to preserve institutions even in weakened form, has helped prevent wider collapse.

Restraint carries a cost. It often goes unnoticed. It can be mistaken for passivity. In moments of anger and despair, it can feel unrewarded. Still, it remains one of the few forces preventing Lebanon's divisions from becoming irreparable.

The Sunni community's relationship with other Lebanese communities reflects its broader condition. Engaged but constrained. Present but cautious. Committed to coexistence without possessing the tools to enforce it.

Although these relationships are not healthy, they remain functional. In Lebanon these days, functionality is survival. The future of intercommunal relations will depend not on dominance by any group, but on whether the state regains enough credibility to matter again.

Until then, Sunnis, Shia, Druze, and Christians will continue to live in proximity, bound less by agreement than by the shared understanding that collapse would spare no one.

Chapter 21

Warning: The Cost of Selective Empathy

Recent years have exposed a growing fracture in how suffering is acknowledged and prioritized in Lebanon's public discourse. This fracture has been especially visible in moments of regional escalation, where violence against Lebanese communities has intersected with international power dynamics. Within this context, the role of Nawaf Salam, a Sunni prime minister has become emblematic of a broader tension rather than an isolated controversy.

Nawaf Salam represents a model of Sunni leadership deeply aligned with international legal norms, Western diplomatic frameworks, and institutional reform language. His background as a jurist and diplomat placed him comfortably within global governance circles. For many Lebanese, this positioning initially signaled competence and reformist promise. For others, particularly within the Shia community, it came to symbolize distance, and government disconnect, not from law, but from lived suffering.

During periods of Israeli military action affecting southern Lebanon and border regions, Shia communities have borne the overwhelming human cost. Homes destroyed, livelihoods disrupted, and civilian deaths have been recurring realities. In these moments, the expectation among many Lebanese was not ideological solidarity, but moral acknowledgment. What emerged instead was a perception of silence, or at best, procedural neutrality.

This perceived disregard did not stem from explicit denial, but from emphasis. Statements framed through international legality, restraint, and balance were read by many as insufficient in the face of asymmetrical violence backed by the United States and broader Western power structures. For Shia communities already skeptical of international institutions, such positioning reinforced the belief that global legal language often fails to protect those most exposed to force.

This perception reverberated beyond the Shia community. Among Sunnis, it deepened an existing tension about representation. Sunni prime ministers, particularly in the post-war and post-2005 eras, have increasingly been viewed, fairly or not, as operating within the orbit of Saudi Arabia and the United States. This perception has hardened over time, shaped by financial dependency, diplomatic alignment, and public rhetoric that prioritizes international approval over domestic consensus.

The label of "stooge" is not a neutral one, but its persistence reveals something important. It reflects the erosion of trust in leadership that appears externally anchored while internally constrained. For many Lebanese, especially those who experience violence or economic deprivation directly, alignment with Western or Gulf powers is no longer seen as protective. It is seen as selective, benefiting some constituencies while leaving others exposed.

This dynamic has placed Sunni leadership in a difficult position. On one hand, engagement with Saudi Arabia and Western governments has historically been essential for economic support, reconstruction, and international legitimacy. On the other, such alignment increasingly carries political cost at home, particularly when it appears to mute response to Israeli violence or American complicity.

The result is not merely intercommunal tension, but moral dissonance. A leadership that speaks the language of reform and legality, but hesitates to confront power when that power inflicts visible harm, risks appearing detached from national suffering. This dissonance has weakened Sunni credibility not only among Shia communities, but also among Sunnis themselves, many of whom question whether international alignment still serves Lebanese interests.

It is important to note that this critique is not a defense of militancy, nor an endorsement of any armed actor. It is a reflection on perception and consequence. In Lebanon, silence is never neutral. It is interpreted through history, imbalance, and memory.

What this moment reveals is the narrowing space for abstraction. Legal language, diplomatic caution, and international alignment no longer satisfy a population living under repeated shock.

Communities now demand acknowledgment before policy, empathy before balance, and clarity before neutrality.

For Sunni leadership, including figures like Nawaf Salam, the challenge ahead is not one of ideology, but of proximity. Proximity to suffering. Proximity to consequence. Proximity to a public that no longer separates foreign policy alignment from domestic responsibility.

Lebanon's fractures are not healed by choosing sides among global powers. They are managed, imperfectly, by recognizing that suffering does not require permission to be named. Any leadership that fails to grasp this risks widening the very divisions it claims to reform.

"Lebanon has an Arab face
and belongs to the Arab world."

Riad al-Solh

Chapter 22

A Community in Transition

The description of the Sunni community in Lebanon as a community in transition is a factual description of a structural shift that has unfolded over time. To understand this transition, one must look not at a single event, but at the gradual erosion of the conditions that once sustained Sunni coherence and influence.

Historically, Sunni communities in Lebanon derived their position from proximity to functioning authority. Their role was shaped by administration, law, commerce, and participation in state institutions. This orientation created continuity as long as governance structures remained stable. Transition began when those structures changed faster than the community's modes of engagement could adapt.

The first source of transition lies in the transformation of the state itself. Empire, mandate, and early independence each provided recognizable pathways to authority. Over time, the Lebanese state lost much of its administrative capacity, predictability, and autonomy. Institutions that once offered continuity became intermittent or ineffective. For a community whose cohesion depended on institutional participation, this shift was foundational.

A second factor is the weakening of collective leadership. Earlier Sunni leadership was dispersed across families, professions, and institutions. Authority was shared and situational. The post-war concentration of power around a limited number of figures altered this pattern. When that concentration collapsed, it did not revert to earlier dispersion. What followed was fragmentation, with no agreed mechanism for regeneration.

Economic transformation further accelerated transition. Urban Sunni life had long relied on public administration, professional sectors, and commercial networks tied to the state. Economic contraction, declining public services, and reduced opportunity weakened these pathways. Migration increased, particularly among younger generations, thinning the social base from which leadership and cohesion had previously emerged.

Social change also plays a role. Educational attainment and professional aspiration remain strong, but traditional routes to stability no longer offer the same outcomes. This has altered expectations and reshaped relationships between leadership and community. Participation persists, but attachment to collective direction has diminished.

Regional dynamics contribute additional pressure. External actors continue to influence Lebanese political life, often reshaping priorities and alliances. Sunni leadership, historically accustomed to operating within sovereign institutions, now navigates a landscape where authority is frequently mediated by forces beyond the state. This further complicates efforts to reestablish continuity.

Importantly, this transition does not imply withdrawal. Sunni communities remain present in cities, active in civic life, and engaged in national processes. What has changed is not presence, but anchoring. The frameworks that once absorbed participation and converted it into coherence now function unevenly or not at all.

The Sunni community is therefore in transition because the environment that shaped it has been transformed. Its historical alignment with governance, while once a strength, now requires recalibration in a context where governance itself is fragile. The transition is structural rather than moral, historical rather than personal.

Describing the community as in transition acknowledges movement rather than outcome. It recognizes that older forms of organization no longer operate as they once did, while new forms have not yet fully taken shape. This condition is neither unique nor permanent. It reflects a moment in a longer historical arc.

Understanding this transition allows the Sunni experience to be read with proportion. It avoids narratives of loss or failure and replaces them with context. It situates the community within Lebanon's broader condition, a country itself in prolonged transition, still negotiating the balance between structure, identity, and continuity.

Chapter 23

What This Transition Means for Lebanon

The story of the Sunnis in Lebanon does not exist on its own. It never has. Their transition reflects something larger, something that has been unfolding across the country for years. To understand what is changing within the Sunni community is, in many ways, to understand what has been changing within Lebanon itself.

For a long time, the Sunnis believed in the state. Not as an idea, but as a working reality. Courts mattered. Ministries and Public offices mattered. The system was imperfect, but it functioned well enough to give meaning to participation. You entered it, served within it, and trusted that it would hold. That trust is what has been eroding.

As institutions weakened, something subtle but profound happened. Roles remained, but authority thinned. Titles survived, but power became harder to locate. Decisions took longer, responsibility became blurred, and the state slowly lost its ability to act with clarity. For a community whose identity had been shaped by governance rather than autonomy, this shift was deeply unsettling.

The Sunni transition reflects this loss of ground. Not a retreat from Lebanon, and not a rejection of the state, but a growing uncertainty about how participation translates into stability. When institutions no longer carry weight, engagement begins to feel symbolic rather than effective.

This is not a uniquely Sunni experience. Other communities have responded differently because their relationship to the state was always different. Some relied on land, others on hierarchy, others on tightly bound structures outside formal governance. The Sunnis relied on institutions. When those institutions weakened, the impact was immediate.

The consequences are visible across the country. Politics becomes reactive. Leadership focuses on managing moments rather than shaping direction. Public trust fades, not because people no longer care, but because they no longer see results. Young people look outward. Families adapt quietly. The rhythm of national life slows into stagnation.

What is often misunderstood is that this transition is not about loss of influence alone. It is about the loss of a shared framework that once gave meaning to participation. When the state stops functioning as a reliable center, communities are left to navigate uncertainty in different ways.

The Sunni transition, then, is not a problem to be solved in isolation. It is a signal. It tells us something about the condition of Lebanon itself. A country cannot remain stable when its institutions exist only on paper, when authority is negotiated endlessly but rarely exercised.

Lebanon has endured and survived because its people, despite everything, continue to believe that the country is worth holding together. The Sunni community remains part of that belief. Still urban. Still engaged. Still invested in the idea that public life matters, even when the system disappoints.

Lebanon's future depends not on redistributing roles, but on restoring confidence in the institutions that bind its people together. Until that happens, his community will continue to adapt, to wait, and to live in transition.

"There is no victory for one Lebanese over another."

Rashid Karami

Chapter 24

My Final Thoughts

The Sunnis of Lebanon have long been a people of institutions of cities. Their history is marked by their proximity to authority and participation in public life. For centuries, they lived close to power, trusting systems, offices, and laws more than geography or arms. This choice shaped both their influence and their vulnerability.

Their story is one of engagement. Where others sought protection in land, lineage, or autonomy, Sunnis sought continuity through governance. Where others built strength through separation, they invested in the state. For long periods, this alignment served them well. It offered stability, access, and relevance. It also bound their fate to institutions that could weaken, shift, or disappear.

In every era, the Sunnis have been read through the moment rather than through history. Their presence in power was mistaken for permanence, their absence for failure. Few paused to recognize that Sunni influence was rarely independent. It flowed through structure rather than domination. When the structure held, they stood firm. When it fractured, they were left exposed.

They have served empires and republics, administered cities and ports, negotiated transitions, and carried the burden of governance more often than the privilege of command. Their leaders, from early urban notables to modern prime ministers, reflected this role, mediators more than conquerors, participants more than masters. Even in moments of prominence, their authority depended on balance, restraint, and legitimacy rather than force.

The post-war era altered this equilibrium. Power concentrated where it had once been dispersed. Patronage replaced institution, and personality replaced continuity. When that concentration collapsed, it left fragmentation rather than succession. What followed was not disappearance, but uncertainty, a community still present in the state, but no longer anchored by it in the same way.

As Lebanon's institutions weakened, the Sunni relationship with the state entered a period of transition. Engagement continued, but confidence eroded. Authority remained in form but thinned in substance. Loyalty outlasted effectiveness. What emerged was not rebellion or withdrawal, but recalibration, often hesitant, often uneven.

Today, the Sunnis of Lebanon remain what they have always been, urban, engaged, and intertwined with the country's public life. They have not retreated from Lebanon, nor have they abandoned its institutions. Now, they navigate a landscape where authority is thinner, opportunity narrower, and cohesion harder to sustain. Economic pressure reshapes cities, youth inherit uncertain pathways, and leadership struggles to renew itself within weakened structures.

In Lebanon's delicate balance, the Sunni experience offers a lesson of a different kind. It reminds the nation that reliance on institutions

requires those institutions to endure, and that participation without resilience carries its own risks.

Their history teaches that power exercised through systems can vanish as quickly as those systems dissolve.

This book, like *The Shia of Lebanon*, *The Druze of Lebanon*, and *The Maronites of Lebanon*, forms part of a larger reflection. Each community carries a distinct relationship to power, memory, and survival. Together, they reveal a country held together not by unity, but by balance, negotiated daily and preserved imperfectly.

Lebanon persists because its people, divided in creed and experience, remain bound by history. As that history continues to unfold, the Sunnis of Lebanon will remain what they have long been, a community shaped by governance, tempered by transition, and woven into the life of the state itself. Their story does not conclude here. It continues wherever institutions are rebuilt, cities endure, and public life still matters.

Key Sunnis Families

&

Figures in Lebanon

Chapter 25

Key Sunnis Families & Figures in Lebanon

The Sunni presence in Lebanon has never been organized around a single lineage or dynastic authority. Instead, influence emerged through families rooted in urban life, commerce, administration, religious scholarship, and public service. Their roles evolved across periods, shaped by the state, the city, and shifting political conditions.

This section does not rank families or figures, nor does it assign uniform positions or intentions. It records presence and historical relevance, recognizing that influence varied by era and circumstance.

Beirut

Beirut served as the principal center of Sunni political, economic, and social life. Many families rose through commerce, municipal leadership, and engagement with state institutions.

The **Salam** family played a central role in Beirut's

political life, particularly during the independence period and the early years of the Lebanese republic, contributing to executive governance and municipal affairs.

The **Solh** family was instrumental in the formation of the Lebanese state. Riad al-Solh's role in independence and early governance left a lasting imprint on Sunni participation in national politics.

The **Beyhum**, **Daouk**, **Itani**, **Sinno**, and **Yafi** families were prominent in commerce, religious endowments, municipal leadership, and professional life, contributing to Beirut's civic and economic development.

The **Hariri** family emerged later, reshaping Sunni political dynamics during the post-war reconstruction period. Rafik Hariri's leadership centralized influence and altered the relationship between Sunni politics, the state, and external actors.

Tripoli

Tripoli developed as a distinct Sunni center with its own political culture, shaped by local leadership and regional conditions.

The **Karami** family dominated Tripoli's political life for decades, producing multiple prime ministers and maintaining influence through popular support and national engagement.

The **Mikati** family rose through business and political participation, reflecting newer forms of leadership tied to economic networks and pragmatic governance.

The **Safadi** and **Kabbara** families also played roles in parliamentary representation and local leadership.

Sidon

Sidon's Sunni leadership reflected a blend of local engagement and national participation.

The **Bizri** family historically influenced municipal and political life, while the **Saad** family became prominent through popular leadership and national representation.

The **Hammoud** family has been associated with religious leadership and social influence within the city.

Other Figures and Urban Lineages

Beyond family structures, individual figures emerged through religious scholarship, the judiciary, diplomacy, and professional life. Sunni muftis, judges, educators, and civil servants contributed to public life without necessarily forming dynastic legacies.

This dispersed pattern of influence distinguished Sunni leadership historically. Authority flowed through institutions and offices rather than lineage alone. As political conditions changed, this dispersion weakened, and centralized leadership became more visible.

Author's Note:

This table records **documented public roles and civic presence**, not hierarchy or moral evaluation. Influence varied by era and circumstance. Inclusion reflects historical relevance, not endorsement. What follows next is a partial list of families and individuals public figures and their roles within the Sunni community in Lebanon.

Key Sunnis Families & Figures in Lebanon

Name	City	Role	Notes
Riad al-Solh (1894–1951)	Beirut	Prime Minister	Principal architect of Lebanese independence; first PM after independence (1943).
Saeb Salam (1905–2000)	Beirut	Prime Minister	Served multiple terms; central Sunni leader in early and mid-republican Lebanon.
Tammam Salam	Beirut	Prime Minister	Served 2014–2016 during prolonged governmental paralysis.
Rafik Hariri (1944–2005)	Beirut / Sidon	Prime Minister	Led post-war reconstruction; centralized Sunni political leadership; assassinated 2005.
Saad Hariri	Beirut / Sidon	Prime Minister	Served multiple terms post-2005; leadership marked by

Name	City	Role	Notes
			fragmentation and external pressure.
Bahia Hariri	Sidon	Member of Parliament	Long-serving MP; prominent role in education, social initiatives, and local leadership.
Fouad Siniora	Sidon	Prime Minister	Served 2005–2009; technocratic governance during a transitional period.
Abdul Hamid Karami (1890–1950)	Tripoli	Prime Minister	Early Sunni national leader; foundational figure in Tripoli politics.
Rashid Karami (1921–1987)	Tripoli	Prime Minister	One of Lebanon's longest-serving PMs; assassinated 1987.
Najib Mikati	Tripoli	Prime Minister	Business-oriented leadership model; served multiple terms.
Salim El-Hoss (1929–2024)	Beirut	Prime Minister	Economist; known for integrity, institutional

Name	City	Role	Notes
			loyalty, and ethical governance.
Riad al-Bizri	Sidon	Minister of Health	Physician and public servant; representative of professional Sunni leadership.
Maarouf Saad (1910–1975)	Sidon	Political Leader	Popular nationalist figure; assassination preceded the civil war.
Osama Saad	Sidon	Member of Parliament	Continued Sidon's political representation.
Sheikh Hassan Khaled (1921–1989)	Beirut	Grand Mufti of the Republic	Head of Dar al-Fatwa; advocate of national unity; assassinated 1989.
Nawaf Salam	Beirut	Prime Minister	Legal scholar and diplomat; former ICJ judge; represents reform-oriented technocratic leadership.

Key Sunni Families in Lebanon

Family	City	Role	Notes
Salam Family	Beirut	Political Leadership	Multi-generation participation in governance and public life.
Solh Family	Beirut	Political Leadership	Central role in independence and early state formation.
Beyhum Family	Beirut	Civic & Municipal Roles	Commerce, municipal leadership, religious endowments.
Daouk Family	Beirut	Civic & Municipal Roles	Public service, commerce, and social institutions.
El-Hoss Family	Beirut	Political Leadership	Associated with ethical governance and public service.
Itani Family	Tripoli	Civic & Religious Roles	Municipal leadership and

Family	City	Role	Notes
			religious endowments.
Karami Family	Tripoli	Political Leadership	Dominant Tripoli family across several decades.
Safadi Family	Tripoli	Parliamentary & Business Roles	Parliamentary representation and economic influence.
Kabbara Family	Tripoli	Parliamentary Roles	Local and national political representation.
Hammoud Family	Sidon	Local Social Leadership	Associated with Sunni civic and social authority in Sidon.
Hariri Family	Sidon	Political Leadership	Local and national political leadership; post-war prominence.
Saad Family	Sidon	Political Leadership	Parliamentary leadership in Sidon.

"We are condemned
to live together."

Saeb Salam

References

Recommended Readings

Akarli, E. D. (1993). *The long peace: Ottoman Lebanon, 1861–1920*. University of California Press.

Fawaz, L. T. (1983). *An occasion for war: Civil conflict in Lebanon and Damascus in 1860*. University of California Press.

Harris, W. (2012). *Lebanon: A history, 600–2011*. Oxford University Press.

Hourani, A. (1983). *Arabic thought in the liberal age, 1798–1939*. Cambridge University Press.

Hourani, A. (1991). *A history of the Arab peoples*. Harvard University Press.

Kassir, S. (2010). *Beirut*. University of California Press.

Makdisi, U. S. (2000). *The culture of sectarianism: Community, history, and violence in nineteenth-century Ottoman Lebanon*. University of California Press.

Salam, S. (1979). *Lebanon reborn.* I. B. Tauris. *(Primary Sunni political perspective)*

Salibi, K. S. (1988). *A house of many mansions: The history of Lebanon reconsidered.* University of California Press.

Traboulsi, F. (2012). *A history of modern Lebanon* (2nd ed.). Pluto Press.

Yamak, L. (1966). *The Lebanese political system.* Oxford University Press.

Zisser, E. (2000). *Lebanon: The challenge of independence.* I. B. Tauris.

About Dr. Abraham Khoureis, Ph.D.

Dr. Abraham Khoureis, Ph.D., is a multi-talented thought leader and partner, author, an award-winning mentor, a global thinker, and advocate for compassionate leadership. He is an adjunct university professor who specializes in teaching graduate-level courses in business and management, blending academic theory with real-world business practices. Dr. Khoureis is also a small business owner and holds numerous state certifications and professional designations and licenses, highlighting his multidisciplinary expertise.

He is the creator of the Compassionate Leadership Model and Pyramid, which emphasizes leadership built on self-awareness, mindfulness, and commitment to serving others without expectation of return. This seven-level model pyramid, with "Community" as its fifth level, reflects his vision of leadership that positively impacts the broader community and society.

Moreover, Dr. Khoureis developed the Disability Learning Attainment Model, a framework designed to empower individuals with disabilities through inclusive education, skill-building, and leadership development. His work champions and empowers inclusivity, accessibility, and ethical practices in both education and leadership. He has been published on *Forbes.com*, *Newsweek.com*, and the distinguished *Leader to Leader Journal*. He was recognized as LinkedIn's Top Leadership and Management Voice, and Thinkers360's Top 50 Voices.

Dr. Abraham's contributions extend to his writings, professional development initiatives, and thought leadership, making him a respected emerging leader in the fields of compassionate leadership, organizational behavior, and human resources development.

Easily accessible at:
DrAbeKhoureis.com – DrAbeBooks.com

Social Media: @DrAbeKhoureis

On Amazon.com, search for Dr. Abraham Khoureis

Other Books by Dr. Abraham Khoureis, Ph.D.

The Shia of Lebanon: The Guardians of the Nation. ISBN: 978-1-966837-35-3

The Druze of Lebanon: The Keepers of the Mountain. ISBN: 978-1-966837-75-6

The Maronites of Lebanon: Identity Crisis, A Divided Nation. ISBN: 978-1-966837-36-7

The Sunnis of Lebanon: A Community in Transition. ISBN: 978-1-966837-38-1

SELF: Introducing The Self Rotating Model. ISBN: 979-8-989521-15-9

The Compassionate Leadership Model and Pyramid. ISBN: 979-8-989521-10-4

For his latest published books:

Visit Amazon.com, search for Dr. Abraham Khoureis

www.ingramcontent.com/pod-product-compliance
Lightning Source LLC
Chambersburg PA
CBHW051925240626
47153CB00004B/1376